THE DAY MY FART FOLLOWED ME TO HOCKEY

Ben Jackson & Sam Lawrence

Illustrated By Danko Herrera

Our inspiration for this book came from our son Finn
who just completed his first hockey tryouts this year.

No matter what we are so proud of you!

Timmy paced back and forth in his room nervously, his hockey stick clutched in his sweaty hand.

"I don't know if I can do this. What if I'm not good enough? What if they laugh at me?" Timmy fretted, wringing his hands

"Why on earth would they laugh, Timmy? You're GREAT!" Little Fart exclaimed. The Little Fart was Timmy's best friend.

Timmy thought back to the day the Little Fart had followed him home from school. Ever since then, they had gone everywhere together.

Well...almost everywhere, whether Timmy wanted him to or not.

"**But you don't get it! I have to try out in front of all my friends. And there will be other kids there, too. Strangers!**" Timmy blurted out.

"**You can do it! I know you can, and I will be right there with you!**" reassured the Little Fart. He loved going on adventures with Timmy.

"**NOOOOO, please. Whatever you do, don't come to hockey with me. That's all I need! Everyone will think I stink!**" Timmy said, turning away. The idea of Little Fart following him around and stinking up the place made him even more nervous.

"**But Timmy, I promise I'll be good. Super good!**" swore the Little Fart.

The next day, Timmy stood outside the arena with his brand-new hockey bag. His mom had bought him a new bag and stick. It was the best stick he had ever had.

"I'm so nervous, Mom. Maybe I should wait until next year when I'm bigger and stronger," stuttered Timmy.

"Timmy, don't worry about it, okay? You will never know unless you try." Timmy's mom gave his hand a squeeze. **"I would rather see you try and fail than never take the chance to see what could happen."**

"Okay, Mom, you're right," Timmy agreed reluctantly, and slowly walked toward the arena.

A bunch of kids were in the dressing room. Timmy sat down and started putting on his hockey equipment. He felt really anxious.

Mom tied the laces tight on his skates. "**Good luck, Timmy,**" she whispered with an encouraging smile before she turned to leave. Timmy found himself alone with the Coach and other kids.

"**Hi, everyone! I want to welcome you all to a new hockey season! My name is Kip. You can call me Coach or Coach Kip, if you like. It's my first year coaching, and I'm really excited, and nervous too. No matter what happens this year, remember one thing! We are here to have fun. So, let's get out there and get started!**" encouraged Coach Kip.

Timmy stepped onto the ice, trying to stay focused and to breathe deeply.

"*Psst.*" Timmy heard a slight noise in the distance. He ignored it, trying to concentrate.

"*PSST!*" came the noise again, this time louder and more insistent.

Timmy's eyes scanned the rink, and then he saw him. "**Oh no....**" Timmy groaned inwardly. The Little Fart was sitting right inside the goalie net, smiling away. Timmy skated around the net, looking in both directions to make sure no one would notice him talking to the empty net. Only Timmy could see his special stinky friend, but others could definitely smell him.

"**Little Fart! What are you doing here?**" hissed Timmy.

"**I came to cheer you on, silly. I'm your best friend, remember?**" the Little Fart smiled.

"Okay.... that's fine I guess. But please, whatever you do, don't follow me around! I can't—no—I WON'T be the stinky kid!" Timmy took off, lining up with the other players.

The coach lined up the players for some skills, tests, and drills. Timmy struggled with some, but did well with others.

During a water break, Timmy stood by the boards near the edge of the ice, not feeling very confident at all. He just wanted to leave.

"Timmy, I know you're feeling nervous right now, but I know you can do this!" exclaimed the Little Fart.

"How would you know? You're just a fart!" Timmy shouted, skating away.

Timmy felt bad immediately. He didn't mean to get angry at Little Fart, but really, what did he know about hockey?

Meanwhile, the Little Fart just sat quietly on the bench. It was very upsetting to see his best friend mad at him. After all, Little Fart was only trying to help.

Suddenly the hopeless feeling of sadness changed to inspiration. The Little Fart had an idea! He had single-handedly come up with a great plan - or so he thought.

Little Fart didn't have a clue what this hockey stuff was all about. All he knew was that Timmy was sad and dressed in funny clothes. He also saw that this place was cold, and the kids shot hard little black things at people. In fact, one of the black things had almost hit him! *I know just what Timmy needs. He needs me to help him,* thought the Little Fart. He smiled as he ran back to the changing rooms.

Timmy was practicing a drill when he looked up to see the Little Fart dressed up in skates, holding a hockey stick. It appeared he had attempted a traditional hockey ensemble, but was way off the mark. He wore a baseball cap, one elbow pad, and a pair of hockey pants.

"**Oh gosh,**" Timmy groaned inwardly, "**this isn't going to end well at all....**"

At this point Timmy felt confused. **"Little Fart, what on earth are you doing?"**

"I'm playing hockey with Timmy! And that makes Timmy happy!" said the Little Fart.

"Well...you clearly don't know what you're doing and you shouldn't be on the ice," Timmy chuckled. **"But I'll admit you are helping with my nerves."** For the first time that day, Timmy began to relax.

"Oh, Little Fart, you're so silly. But how is making me happy going to improve my game? These other kids are really good. If I don't start playing better and stand out to the Coach, there is no way I'm going to make the team."

The Little Fart thought hard.

"Timmy, I've got it!" Little Fart skated off, wobbling across the ice toward the other players.

"Got what? What's the plan?" shouted Timmy, confused.

"You'll see, Timmy!" shouted the Little Fart, as he began to weave in, out, and around the kids on the rink. Timmy didn't know what was going on, but he started to get an idea when he saw the looks on the kids' faces. It was clear they smelled something funny—no, not funny—**farty**!

Timmy couldn't help but laugh! The kids tried to drift away from each other with sour expressions, wanting to avoid the person who had farted.

"**Whoever denied it, supplied it!**" another boy yelled out from across the ice.

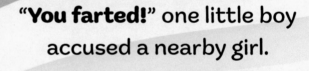

"**You farted!**" one little boy accused a nearby girl.

"Whoever smelt it, dealt it!" she shouted back.

"Well, whoever made the rhyme, committed the crime!" Timmy called, joining in with the other kids. Before long, every kid out on the ice was rolling with laughter over the fart rhymes. It got so out of hand that Coach had to blow his whistle three times to get the kids back on track.

After that, Timmy finally relaxed and started to have fun. He began to pass the skills tests and drills. He owed it all to his best friend, the Little Fart!

At the end of tryouts, Coach Kip called all the players to the center of the ice.

"Well done, everyone! I am pleased to inform you that you all made the team!" the Coach announced, beaming. **"Now, go and get changed, and I'll see you all next week."**

The players cheered and high-fived as they skated toward the locker room.

Timmy didn't follow the other kids in their celebration. He had something else to do first. Instead, he found his biggest fan, stinking and clapping on the bench.

"Sorry for snapping at you, Little Fart. I know you were only trying to help. And thanks to you, I made the team!"

"**That's great! And don't worry about it. I know you just needed a little help. That's what friends are for, Timmy!**" the Little Fart said, jumping into Timmy's arms and hugging him tightly.

"**Who would have thought the kids smelling my fart would help me make the hockey team?**" Timmy laughed. "**Come on, buddy, Mom's taking us out for ice cream.**"

The two skated off to the locker room hand-in-hand, just a little hockey player and his Little Fart.

What kind of exciting adventure would they have next?

Note From The Authors

As Indie authors, we work hard to produce high-quality work for the enjoyment of all our readers. If you can spare one minute, please leave a review of our book. We would greatly appreciate it! Let everyone know just how much you and your children enjoyed Timmy and his Fart! We are currently working on expanding this series, so stay tuned for future updates by following us on Amazon. Check out our Facebook page or website for more updates.

www.facebook.com/benandsamauthors & www.benandsamauthors.com

Thank you, Ben and Sam

Author Page Ben and Sam

Ben and Sam currently live in Ontario, Canada, and Tasmania, Australia. Ben was born in Tasmania, Australia, while Sam was born in Toronto, Canada. Between the two of them, they enjoy travelling frequently, and they both have two children. With their three boys and one girl, they both enjoy spending quality time with their families, reading books, playing games, and exploring both Canada and Australia.

Other Books by Ben & Sam

My Little Fart Series

The Day My Fart Followed Me Home
The Day My Fart Followed Me To Hockey
The Day My Fart Followed Santa Up The Chimney
The Day My Fart Followed Me To Soccer
The Day My Fart Followed Me To The Dentist
The Day My Fart Followed Me To The Zoo
The Day My Fart Followed Me To Baseball
The Day My Fart Followed Me To The Hospital
It's Not Easy Being A Little Fart

If I Was A Caterpillar
Don't Fart in the Pool

Hockey Wars Series

Hockey Wars
Hockey Wars 2 - The New Girl
Hockey Wars 3 - The Tournament
Hockey Wars 4 - Championships
Hockey Wars 5 - Lacrosse Wars
Hockey Wars 6 - Middle School
Hockey Wars 7 - Winter Break
Hockey Wars 8 - Spring Break
Hockey Wars 9 - Summer Camp
Hockey Wars 10 - State Tryouts
Hockey Wars 11 - State Tournament

Made in the USA
Middletown, DE
08 February 2023